# insectAsides

**OTHERBOOKS BY martha paulos:**
*Doggerel*
and
*Felines*

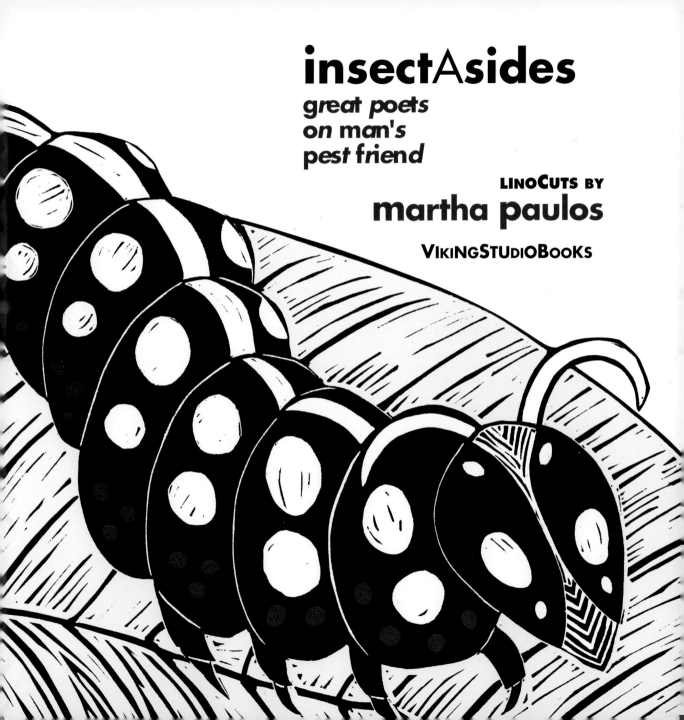

# insectAsides

*great poets
on man's
pest friend*

LinoCuts by

## martha paulos

VikingStudioBooks

**VIKING STUDIO BOOKS**

Published by the Penguin Group • Penguin Books USA Inc., 375 Hudson Street, New York 10014, U.S.A. • Penguin Books Ltd, 27 Wrights Lane, London W8 5TZ, England • Penguin Books Australia Ltd, Ringwood, Victoria, Australia • Penguin Books Canada Ltd, 10 Alcorn Avenue, Toronto, Ontario, Canada M4V 3B2 • Penguin Books (N.Z.) Ltd, 182-190 Wairau Road, Auckland 10, New Zealand • Penguin Books Ltd, Registered Offices: Harmondsworth, Middlesex, England

First published in 1994 by Viking Penguin, a division of Penguin Books USA Inc.

10  9  8  7  6  5  4  3  2  1

Grateful acknowledgment is made for permission to publish the following copyrighted works:

"A Considerable Speck" by Robert Frost from *The Poetry of Robert Frost*, edited by Edward Connery Lathem. Copyright 1942 by Robert Frost. Copyright © 1970 by Lesley Frost Ballantine. Copyright © 1969 by Henry Holt and Company, Inc. Reprinted by permission of Henry Holt and Company, Inc.

"The Flattered Lightening Bug" by Don Marquis from *Archy and Mehitabel* by Don Marquis. Copyright 1927 by Doubleday, a division of Bantam, Doubleday, Dell Publishing Group, Inc. Reprinted by permission of Doubleday, a division of Bantam, Doubleday, Dell Publishing Group, Inc.

"r-p-o-p-h-e-s-s-a-g-r" by E. E. Cummings from *Complete Poems, 1904-1962* by E . E . Cummings, edited by George J. Firmage. Copyright © 1935, 1963, 1991 by the Trustees for the E. E. Cummings Trust. Reprinted by permission of Liveright Publishing Corporation.

"Mosquitoes" by José Emilio Pacheco from *Don't Ask Me How The Time Goes By* by José Emilio Pacheco. translated by Alastair Reid. Copyright © 1978 by Columbia University Press, New York. Reprinted by permission of the publisher.

"The Ant" by Ogden Nash from *Verses From 1929 On* by Ogden Nash. Copyright 1935 by Ogden Nash. First appeared in *The Saturday Evening Post*. Reprinted by permission of Little, Brown and Company.

"Insect Heads" by Robert Bly from *This Tree Will Be Here For A Thousand Years* by Robert Bly. Copyright © 1979 by Robert Bly. Reprinted by permission of HarperCollins Publishers, Inc.

"The Spider holds a Silver Ball" by Emily Dickinson from *The Poems of Emily Dickinson* by Thomas H Johnson, ed., Cambridge, Mass.: The Belknap Press of Harvard University Press. Copyright © 1951, 1955, 1979, 1983 by the President and Fellows of Harvard College. Reprinted by permission of the publishers and the Trustees of Amherst College.

"Insects Noir" by Herbert Mitgang. Copyright © 1994 by Herbert Mitgang. Published by arrangement with the author.

"The Arrival of the Bee Box" by Sylvia Plath from *Ariel* by Sylvia Plath. Copyright © 1963 by Ted Hughes. Reprinted by permission of HarperCollins Publishers, Inc. and Faber and Faber Ltd.

Selection (titled "Fleas Interest Me So Much") from *Bestiary/Bestiario: A Poem by Pablo Neruda*, translated by Elsa Neuberger. Copyright © 1965 and renewed 1993 by Harcourt Brace & Company. Reprinted by permission of Harcourt Brace & Company.

**ISBN** 0-670-85567-7
CIP data available.

Printed in Singapore

**To Clark,**

**who found lots of bugs for me to draw,**
**and to all those brave insects**
**who gave their lives**
**for this book.**

# contents

# christopher morley

## dedicated to don marquis

Scuttle, scuttle, little roach —
How you run when I approach:
Up above the pantry shelf.
Hastening to secrete yourself.

Most adventurous of vermin,
How I wish I could determine
How you spend your hours of ease,
Perhaps reclining on the cheese.

Cook has gone, and all is dark —
Then the kitchen is your park:
In the garbage heap that she leaves
Do you browse among the tea leaves?

How delightful to suspect
All the places you have trekked:
Does your long antenna whisk its
Gentle tip across the biscuits?

Do you linger, little soul,
Drowsing in our sugar bowl?
Or, abandonment most utter,
Shake a shimmy on the butter?

Do you chant your simple tunes
Swimming in the baby's prunes?
Then, when dawn comes, do you slink
Homeward to the kitchen sink?

Timid roach, why be so shy?
We are brothers, thou and I.
In the midnight, like yourself,
I explore the pantry shelf!

# william wordsworth

## to a butterfly

I've watched you now a full half-hour,
Self-poised upon that yellow flower;
And, little Butterfly! indeed
I know not if you sleep or feed.
How motionless! — not frozen seas
More motionless! and then
What joy awaits you, when the breeze
Hath found you out among the trees,
And calls you forth again!

This plot of orchard-ground is ours;
My trees they are, my Sister's flowers;
Here rest your wings when they are weary;
Here lodge as in a sanctuary!

P. rarae

Clarkus

H. Comma

Phoebeus

C. Croeus

A. Idalia

Lillaus

Carmena

A. Dollia

M. Phaeton

Zoeus

Alexus

Hannae

Come often to us, fear no wrong;
Sit near us on the bough!
We'll talk of sunshine and of song,
And summer days, when we were young;
Sweet childish days, that were as long
As twenty days are now.

# robert frost

## a considerable speck

A speck that would have been beneath my sight
On any but a paper sheet so white
Set off across what I had written there.
And I had idly poised my pen in air
To stop it with a period of ink
When something strange about it made me think.
This was no dust speck by my breathing blown,
But unmistakably a living mite
With inclinations it could call its own.
It paused as with suspicion of my pen,
And then came racing wildly on again
To where my manuscript was not yet dry;
Then paused again and either drank or smelt —
With loathing, for again it turned to fly.

Plainly with an intelligence I dealt.
It seemed too tiny to have room for feet,
Yet must have had a set of them complete
To express how much it didn't want to die.
It ran with terror and with cunning crept.
It faltered; I could see it hesitate;
Then in the middle of the open sheet
Cower down in desperation to accept
Whatever I accorded it of fate.

I have none of the tenderer-than-thou
Collectivistic regimenting love
With which the modern world is being swept.
But this poor microscopic item now!
Since it was nothing I knew evil of
I let it lie there till I hope it slept.

I have a mind myself and recognize
Mind when I meet with it in any guise.
No one can know how glad I am to find
On any sheet the least display of mind.

# don marquis

## the flattered lightning bug

a lightning bug got
in here the other night a
regular hick from
the real country he was
awful proud of himself you
city insects may think
you are some punkins
but i don t see any
of you flashing in the dark
like we do in
the country all right go
to it says i mehitabel the
cat and that green
spider who lives in your locker

and two or three cockroach
friends of mine and a
friendly rat all gathered
around him and urged him on
and he lightened and
lightened and lightened you
don t see anything like this
in town often he says go to it
we told him it s a
real treat to us and
we nicknamed him broadway
which pleased him
this is the life
he said all i
need is a harbor
under me to be a
statue of liberty and
he got so vain of
himself I had to take
him down a peg you ve

made lightning for two hours
little bug i told him
but i don t hear
any claps of thunder
yet there are some men
like that when he wore
himself out mehitabel
the cat ate him

— archy

14

# ralph waldo emerson

## the humble-bee

Burly, dozing humble-bee,
Where thou art is clime for me.
Let them sail for Porto Rique,
Far-off heats through seas to seek;
I will follow thee alone,
Thou animated torrid-zone!
Zigzag steerer, desert cheerer,
Let me chase thy waving lines;
Keep me nearer, me thy hearer,
Singing over shrubs and vines.

Insect lover of the sun,
Joy of thy dominion!
Sailor of the atmosphere;

Swimmer through the waves of air;
Voyager of light and noon;
Epicurean of June;
Wait, I prithee, till I come
Within earshot of thy hum, —
All without is martyrdom.

When the south wind, in May days,
With a net of shining haze
Silvers the horizon wall,
And, with softness touching all,
Tints the human countenance
With a color of romance,
And, infusing subtle heats,
Turns the sod to violets,
Thou, in sunny solitudes,
Rover of the underwoods,
The green silence dost displace
With thy mellow, breezy bass.

Hot midsummer's petted crone,
Sweet to me thy drowsy tone
Tells of countless sunny hours,
Long days, and solid banks of flowers;
Of gulfs of sweetness without bound
In Indian wildernesses found;
Of Syrian peace, immortal leisure,
Firmest cheer, and bird-like pleasure.

Aught unsavory or unclean
Hath my insect never seen;
But violets and bilberry bells,
Maple-sap and daffodels,
Grass with green flag half-mast high,
Succory to match the sky,
Columbine with horn of honey,
Scented fern, and agrimony,
Clover, catchfly, adder's-tongue
And brier-roses, dwelt among;
All besides was unknown waste,
All was picture as he passed.

Wiser far than human seer,
Yellow-breeched philosopher!
Seeing only what is fair,
Sipping only what is sweet,
Thou dost mock at fate and care,
Leave the chaff and take the wheat
When the fierce northwestern blast
Cools sea and land so far and fast,
Thou already slumberest deep;
Woe and want thou canst outsleep;
Want and woe, which torture us,
Thy sleep makes ridiculous.

# christina rossetti

## the caterpillar

Brown and furry
Caterpillar in a hurry,
Take your walk
To the shady leaf, or stalk,
Or what not,
Which may be the chosen spot.
No toad spy you,
Hovering bird of prey pass by you;
Spin and die,
To live again a butterfly.

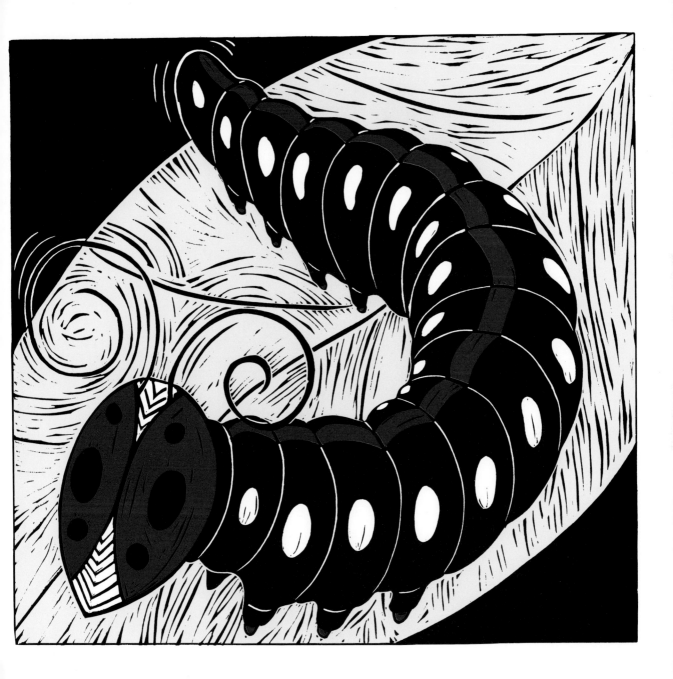

# william blake

## the fly

Little fly,
Thy summer's play
My thoughtless hand
Has brushed away.

Am not I
A fly like thee?
Or art not thou
A man like me?

For I dance
And drink and sing,
Till some blind hand
Shall brush my wing.

If thought is life
And strength and breath,
And the want
Of thought is death,

Then am I
A happy fly,
If I live
Or if I die.

# e. e. cummings

**r-p-o-p-h-e-s-s-a-g-r**

r-p-o-p-h-e-s-s-a-g-r
who

a)s w(e loo)k
upnowgath
               PPEGORHRASS

                              eringint(o-
aThe):l
       eA
          !p:
S                                          a
            (r
rIvInG      .gRrEaPsPhOs)
                           to
rea(be)rran(com)gi(e)ngly
,grasshopper;

# robert burns

## to a louse

Ha! whare ye gaun, ye crowlin' ferlie?
Your impudence protects you sairly;
I canna say but ye strunt rarely
Owre gauze and lace,
Tho' faith! I fear ye dine but sparely
On sic a place.

Ye ugly, creepin', blastit wonner,
Detested, shunned by saunt an' sinner,
How daur ye set your fit upon her —
Sae fine a lady!
Gae somewhere else and seek your dinner
On some poor body.

Swith! in some begger's hauffet squattle:
There ye may creep and sprawl and sprattle,
Wi' ither kindred, jumping cattle,
In shoals and nations;
Whare horn nor bane ne'er daur unsettle
Your thick plantations.

Now haud you there! ye're out o' sight,
Below the fatt'rils, snug an' tight;
Na, faith ye yet! ye'll no be right
Till ye've got on it —
The vera tapmost, tow'ring height
O' Miss's bonnet.

My sooth! right bauld ye set your nose out,
As plump an' grey as onie grozet;
O for some rank, mercurial rozet;
Or fell red smeddum,
I'd gie ye sic a hearty dose o't,
Wad dress your droddum.

I wad na been surprised to spy
You on an auld wife's flainen toy;
Or aiblins some bit duddie boy,
On 's wyliecoat;
But Miss's fine Lunardi! fye!
How daur ye do't?

O Jenny, dinna toss your head,
An' set your beauties a' abread!
Ye little ken what cursèd speed
The blastie's makin'!
Thae winks an' finger-ends, I dread,
Are notice takin'!

O wad some Power the giftie gie us
To see oursels as ithers see us!
It wad frae monie a blunder free us,
An' foolish notion;
What airs in dress an' gait wad lea'e us,
An' ev'n devotion!

# william roscoe

## the butterfly's ball and the grasshopper's feast

Come, take up your hats, and away let us haste
To the Butterfly's ball and the Grasshopper's feast;
The trumpeter Gad-fly has summon'd the crew,
And the revels are now only waiting for you.

On the smooth-shaven grass by the side of the wood,
Beneath a broad oak that for ages has stood,
See the children of earth, and tenants of air,
For an evening's amusement together repair.

And there came the Beetle, so blind and so black,
Who carried the Emmet, his friend, on his back;
And there came the Gnat, and the Dragon-fly too,
And all their relations, green, orange, and blue.

And there came the Moth with her plumage of down,

And the Hornet with jacket of yellow and brown.
Who with him the Wasp, his companion, did bring;
They promised that evening to lay by their sting.

Then the sly little Dormouse peep'd out of his hole,
And led to the feast his blind cousin the Mole;
And the Snail, with his horns peeping out from his shell,
Came fatigued with the distance, the length of an ell.

A mushroom the table, and on it were spread
A Water-dock-leaf, which their table-cloth made;
The viands were various, to each of their taste,
And the Bee brought the honey to sweeten the feast.

With steps more majestic the Snail did advance,
And he promised the gazers a minuet dance;
But they all laughed so loudly he pulled in his head,
And went in his own little chamber to bed.

Then, as evening gave way to the shadows of night,
Their watchman, the Glow-worm, came out with his light:
So home let us hasten, while yet we can see,
For no watchman is waiting for you or for me.

# josé emilio pacheco

## mosquitoes

They are born in the swamps of sleeplessness.
They are a viscous blackness which wings about.
Little frail vampires,
miniature dragonflies,
small picadors
with the devil's own sting.

# ogden nash

## the ant

The ant has made himself illustrious
Through constant industry industrious.
So what?
Would you be calm and placid
If you were full of formic acid?

# robert bly

## insect heads

Those insects, golden
and Arabic, sailing in the husks of galleons,
their octagonal heads also
hold sand paintings of the next life.

# emily dickinson

## the spider holds a silver ball

The Spider holds a Silver Ball
In unperceived Hands —
And dancing softly to Himself
His Yarn of Pearl — unwinds —

He plies from Nought to Nought —
In unsubstantial Trade —
Supplants our Tapestries with His —
In half the period —

An Hour to rear supreme
His Continents of Light —
Then dangle from the Housewife's Broom —
His Boundaries — forgot —

# herbert mitgang

## insects noir

Mine can bite, yours get bitten,
By bugeyed flies, I am smitten,
In the realm of living thingies,
Cherish God's small bugs and beasties.

Can a stick of yellow butter fly?
No; but I've watched a monarch butterfly,
Winging its wings across a yellow sky.
Instead of pinning down a butterfly's whisker,
Better butterfly-net a lepidopterister.

Is it cricket to cock a snook
At a cricket's raucous puke?
Should a praying mantis prey

Upon a praying mantis, praying?
I say, no way-ing.

"Where the bee sucks, there suck I,"
Said Master Will in honeyed words,
To which your humble servant only adds
This modest rhyme found in his bonnet:
Honor the queenly mother bee,
For unlike you and certainly me,
She's never committed larceny.

L'envoi:
An alageroo for all earthbound crawly creatures,
Centipedes and caterpillars, katydids and katydidn'ts.
Though honestly bugged by the indomitable roach
(not to mention ticks and flatfoot floozy fleas),
I vow never to say gnuts to gnats, in this reproach.

# sylvia plath

## the arrival of the bee box

I ordered this, this clean wood box
Square as a chair and almost too heavy to lift.
I would say it was the coffin of a midget
Or a square baby
Were there not such a din in it.

The box is locked, it is dangerous.
I have to live with it overnight
And I can't keep away from it.
There are no windows, so I can't see what is in there.
There is only a little grid, no exit.

I put my eye to the grid.
It is dark, dark,

With the swarmy feeling of African hands
Minute and shrunk for export,
Black on black, angrily clambering.

How can I let them out?
It is the noise that appalls me most of all,
The unintelligible syllables.
It is like a Roman mob,
Small, taken one by one, but my god, together!

I lay my ear to furious Latin.
I am not a Caesar.
I have simply ordered a box of maniacs.
They can be sent back.
They can die, I need feed them nothing, I am the owner.

I wonder how hungry they are.
I wonder if they would forget me
If I just undid the locks and stood back and turned into a tree.
There is the laburnum, its blond colonnades,
And the petticoats of the cherry.

They might ignore me immediately
In my moon suit and funeral veil.
I am no source of honey
So why should they turn on me?
Tomorrow I will be sweet God, I will set them free.

The box is only temporary.

# edward lear

## there was an old man in a tree

There was an Old Man in a tree,
Who was horribly bored by a Bee;
When they said, "Does it buzz?"
He replied, "Yes, it does!
It's a regular brute of a Bee!"

# pablo neruda

## fleas interest me so much

Fleas interest me so much
that I let them bite me for hours.
They are perfect, ancient, Sanskrit,
machines that admit of no appeal.
They do not bite to eat,
they bite only to jump;
they are the dancers of the celestial sphere,
delicate acrobats
in the softest and most profound circus;
let them gallop on my skin,
divulge their emotions,
amuse themselves with my blood,
but someone should introduce them to me.
I want to know them closely,
I want to know what to rely on.

# bE

# bEttEr-buggEd

# by thE bEst